Veterinarians /

2.8   0.5

MW01041535

DISCARD

07-08 Follett

Veterinarians

A Level Three Reader

By Charnan Simon

Content Adviser: Eve C. Larocca,
Executive Director Illinois State Veterinary Medical Association

The
Child's
World®

Published by The Child's World®
P.O. Box 326
Chanhassen, MN 55317-0326
800-599-READ
www.childsworld.com

Photo Credits
© Chris Collins/CORBIS: 6
© David Young-Wolff/PhotoEdit: 5
© Jim Craigmyle/CORBIS: 9
© Kathi Lamm/Tony Stone: 13
© Kaz Mori/The ImageBank: 25
© Kelly-Mooney/CORBIS: 3
© LWA-JDC/CORBIS: cover, 14
© Michael Newman/PhotoEdit: 29
© Nancy Sheehan/PhotoEdit: 10
© Richard T. Nowitz/CORBIS: 26
© Royalty-Free/CORBIS: 17
© Tim Wright/CORBIS: 21
© Tom Stewart/CORBIS: 18
© Werner Bokelberg/The Imagebank: 22

Editorial Directions, Inc.: E. Russell Primm and Emily J. Dolbear, Editors;
Alice K. Flanagan, Photo Researcher

The Child's World®: Mary Berendes, Publishing Director

Library of Congress Cataloging-in-Publication Data
Simon, Charnan.
  Veterinarians / by Charnan Simon.
    p. cm. — (Wonder books)
Summary: A simple look at what veterinarians do, the tools they use, and what their
typical day is like.
ISBN 1-56766-492-X (lib. bdg. : alk. paper)
1. Veterinarians—Juvenile literature. 2. Veterinary medicine—Vocational
guidance—Juvenile literature. [1. Veterinarians. 2. Veterinary medicine. 3. Occupations.]
I. Title. II. Wonder books (Chanhassen, Minn.)
SF756.S56 2003
  636.089'023—dc21
  2002151621

Have you ever had a pet? Then you might have visited a veterinarian!

A veterinarian is a doctor who takes care of animals. Sometimes veterinarians are called vets. Vets help animals stay healthy, just as doctors help people stay healthy.

A bird called a cockatiel rests on this vet's hand. →

Many vets have offices where people bring their pets. The people stay with their pets in the waiting room until it is their turn. There are many kinds of animals in the waiting room!

A puppy and a kitten sit in a vet's waiting room.

Healthy animals need **checkups**— just like people. The vet takes the animal's **temperature** and listens to its heart. She looks in its eyes and ears. She examines its teeth. Sometimes she gives the animal **medicine** to keep it from getting sick.

A vet shows a boy how to look in his cat's ears. →

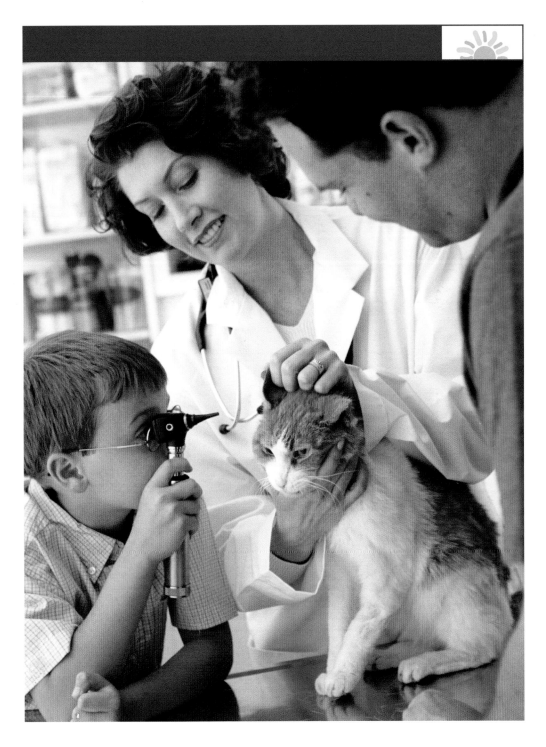

Young animals, like puppies and kittens, need special care. Hold still, puppy! The vet wants to see how much you weigh. He makes sure that the puppy is eating healthy foods.

This newborn puppy lies on a scale.

Taking a blood **sample** is one way to see if an animal is healthy. Checking for fleas and worms is another. This vet talks to a kitten's owners. He makes sure they know how to care for their pet.

A vet speaks to a kitten's owners. →

13

Sometimes animals need more than just checkups. They might be very sick. They might have a broken bone. These animals need to spend the night in the vet's hospital.

This dog has a broken bone.

Vets have special cages for animals that need to stay overnight. The animals can rest here until they are well enough to go home. The vets and their assistants watch over the sick animals very carefully.

This puppy spends the night at the vet's hospital. →

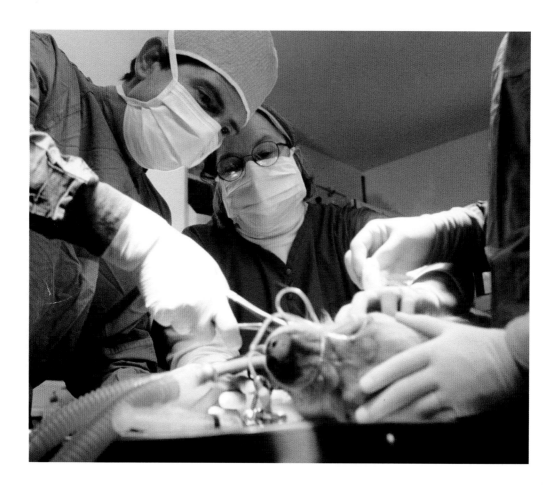

Sometimes animals need **surgery**. The vet gives the animal special medicine so it will sleep through the surgery. The animal needs time after surgery to rest and get better.

Not all veterinarians work in offices. Some vets drive around to farms and stables. They take care of large animals such as cows, horses, sheep, and pigs. Traveling vets carry all the tools and medicines they need with them.

A vet looks at a farmer's piglets. →

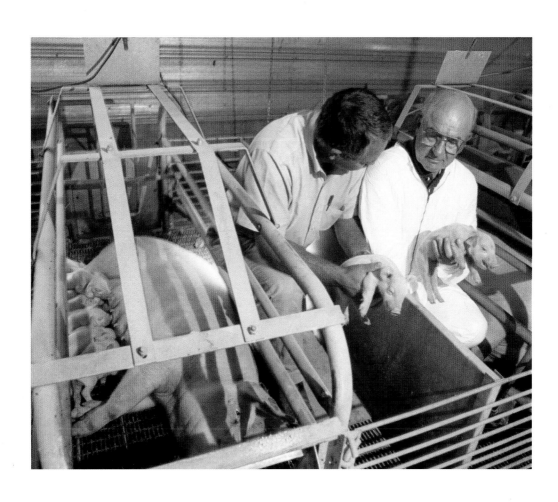

Some vets work in zoos. Elephants and flamingos and dolphins need checkups, too. Polar bears and monkeys and lions can get sick. Sometimes these animals need help giving birth.

This veterinarian holds a lion cub from a zoo.

It takes a long time to become a veterinarian. First you have to study at a college or university. Then you have to go to veterinary school for four years. Students will learn about all kinds of animals. They also train with real veterinarians.

A student learns about an iguana from a vet. →

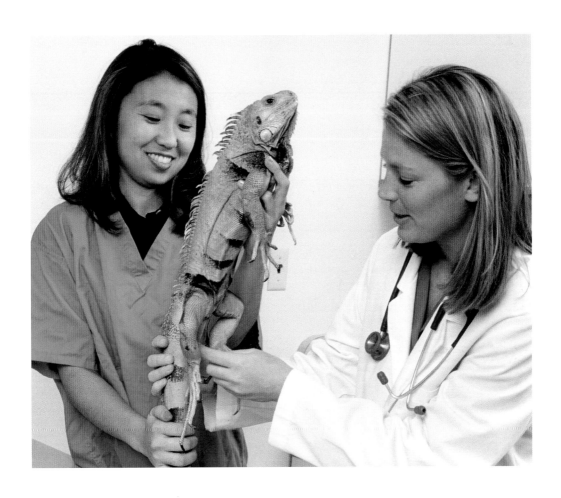

Veterinarians must love animals. They must be smart. Animals can't tell the vet where it hurts. A good vet knows other ways to find out what's wrong.

This veterinarian tries to find out what's wrong with this dolphin.

27

Veterinarians help pets and other animals stay healthy. Vets teach people how to take care of their animals. Being a vet is a rewarding job!

A vet gives this dog a hug! →

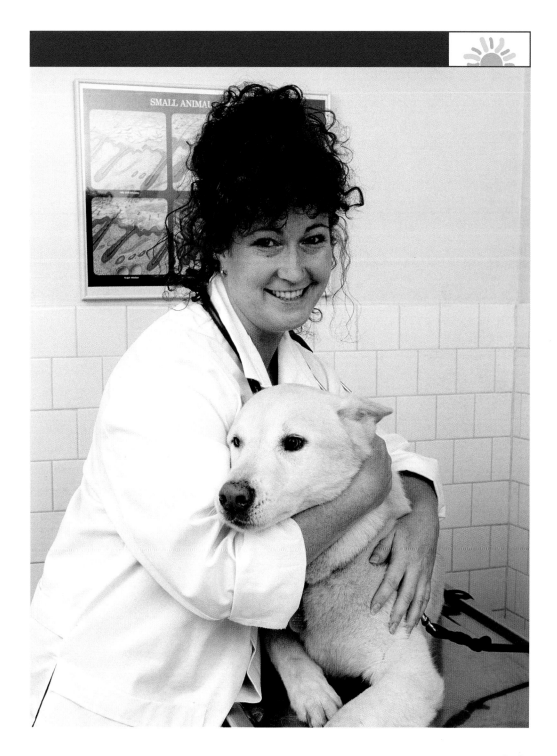

29

Glossary

checkups (CHEK-uhpz)
Checkups are regular visits to a doctor to make sure everything is fine.

medicine (MED-ih-sehn)
Medicine is a drug used to treat illnesses.

sample (SAM-puhl)
A sample is a small amount of something that shows what the whole of it is like.

surgery (SUR-jer-ee)
Surgery is opening the body to find out and fix a health problem.

temperature (TEM-pur-uh-chur)
Your temperature tells how hot or cold your body is.

Index

To Find Out More

Books

Gibbons, Gail. *Say Woof!: The Day of a Country Veterinarian.* New York: Macmillan Publishing Co., 1992.

Maze, Stephanie. *I Want to Be a Veterinarian.* New York: Harcourt, 1999.

Raatma, Lucia. *Veterinarians.* Minneapolis: Compass Point Books, 2003.

Web Sites

Visit our homepage for lots of links about veterinarians:
http://www.childsworld.com/links.html

Note to Parents, Teachers, and Librarians:
We routinely verify our Web links to make sure they're safe, active sites—so encourage your readers to check them out!

Note to Parents and Educators

Welcome to Wonder Books®! These books provide text at three different levels for beginning readers to practice and strengthen their reading skills. Additionally, the use of nonfiction text provides readers the valuable opportunity to *read to learn*, not just to learn to read.

These leveled readers allow children to choose books at their level of reading confidence and performance. Nonfiction Level One books offer beginning readers simple language, word choice, and sentence structure as well as a word list. Nonfiction Level Two books feature slightly more difficult vocabulary, longer sentences, and longer total text. In the back of each Nonfiction Level Two book are an index and a list of books and Web sites for finding out more information. Nonfiction Level Three books continue to extend word choice and length of text. In the back of each Nonfiction Level Three book are a glossary, an index, and a list of books and Web sites for further research.

State and national standards in reading and language arts emphasize using nonfiction at all levels of reading development. Wonder Books® fill the historical void in nonfiction material for primary grade readers with the additional benefit of a leveled text.

About the Author

Charnan Simon lives in Madison, Wisconsin, with her husband and two daughters. She began her publishing career in the children's book division of Little, Brown and Company, and then became an editor of *Cricket Magazine*. Simon is currently a contributing editor for *Click Magazine* and an author with more than 40 books to her credit. When she is not busy writing, she enjoys reading, gardening, and spending time with her family.